W9-CBG-673

I SPY
TWO EYES

— Numbers In Art —

For Walter and Molly

F O R E W O R D

When my own children were tiny, they loved looking at the pictures in a book of medieval paintings. They were fascinated by the minute details and the rich colors and patterns. Over the years we have looked at hundreds of pictures from all over the world, and I hope you will enjoy the twenty I have chosen for this book. They are all paintings except for one, which is a beautiful Japanese woodblock print.

I dedicate this book to my children, without whom I would never have thought of it.

Lucy Micklethwait, 1992

I SPY TWO EYES

— Numbers In Art —

Devised & selected by Lucy Micklethwait

A Mulberry Paperback Book • New York

I spy
one fly

1

Swabian School, *Portrait of a Woman of the Hofer Family*

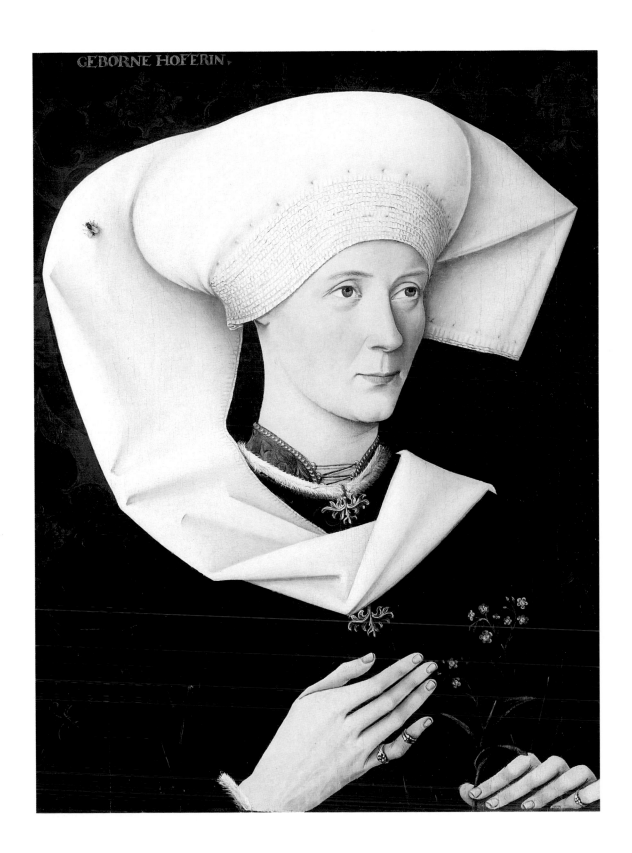
GEBORNE HOFERIN.

I spy
two eyes

2

Karel Appel, *Cry for Freedom*

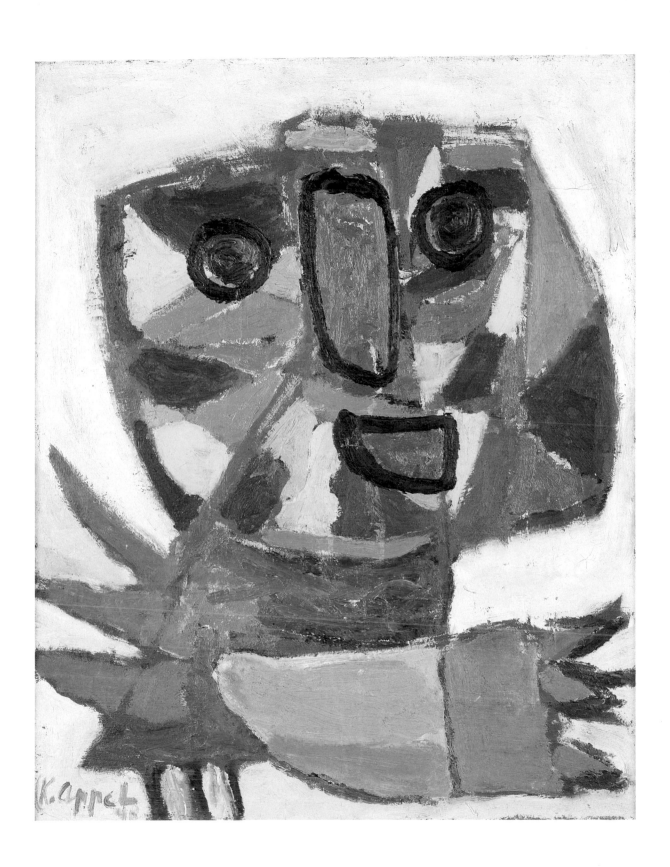

I spy
three puppies

3

Paul Gauguin, *Still Life with Three Puppies* (1888)

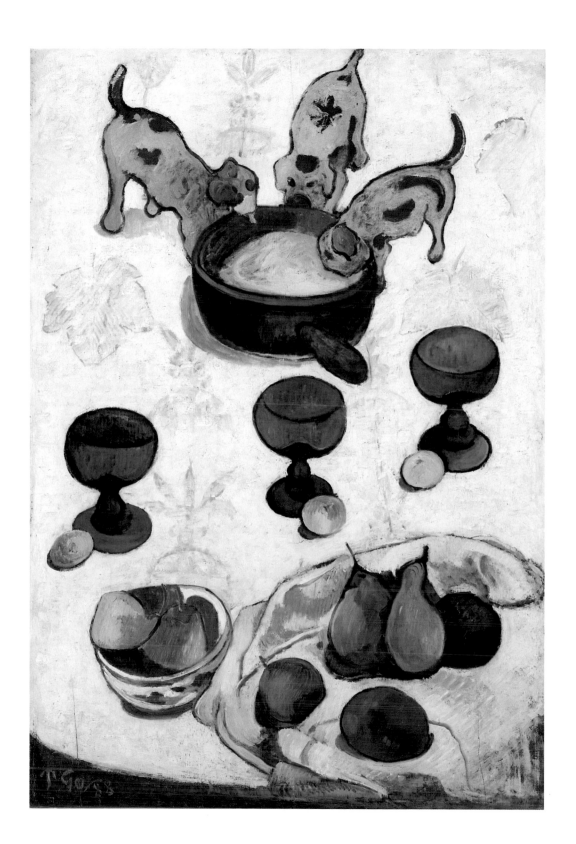

I spy
four fish

4

Henri Matisse, *Goldfish*

I spy
five eggs

5

Jan van Huijsum, *Flowers in a Terracotta Vase*

I spy
six ducks

6

Utagawa Kuniyoshi, *Boat Trip in Winter*

I spy
seven circles

7

Wassily Kandinsky, *Swinging*

I spy
eight boats

8

Vincent Van Gogh, *Boats on the Beach*

I spy
nine children

9

Studio of Peter Paul Rubens, *The Gerbier Family*

I spy
ten hens

10

Sir Stanley Spencer, *St. Francis and the Birds*

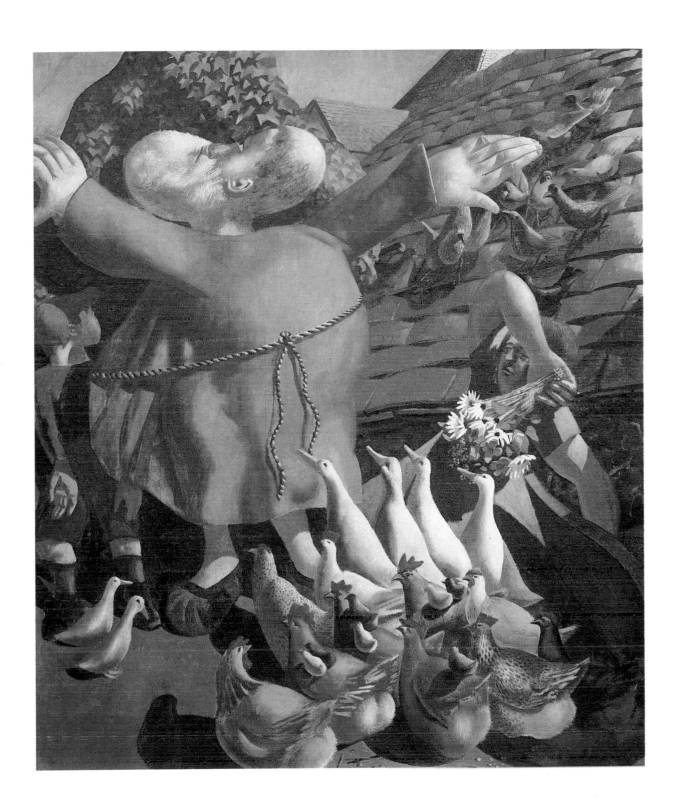

I spy
eleven hares

11

Unknown artist, *The Emblem of the Hare*

I spy
twelve squirrels

12

Abu'l Hasan, *Squirrels in a Plane Tree*

I spy
thirteen singers

13

Thomas Cooper Gotch, *Alleluia*

I spy
fourteen soldiers

14

Henri Rousseau, *Artillerymen*

I spy
fifteen hands and feet

15

Fernand Léger, *Divers on a Yellow Background*

I spy
sixteen apples

16

Lucas Cranach the Elder, *Madonna and Child under an Apple Tree*

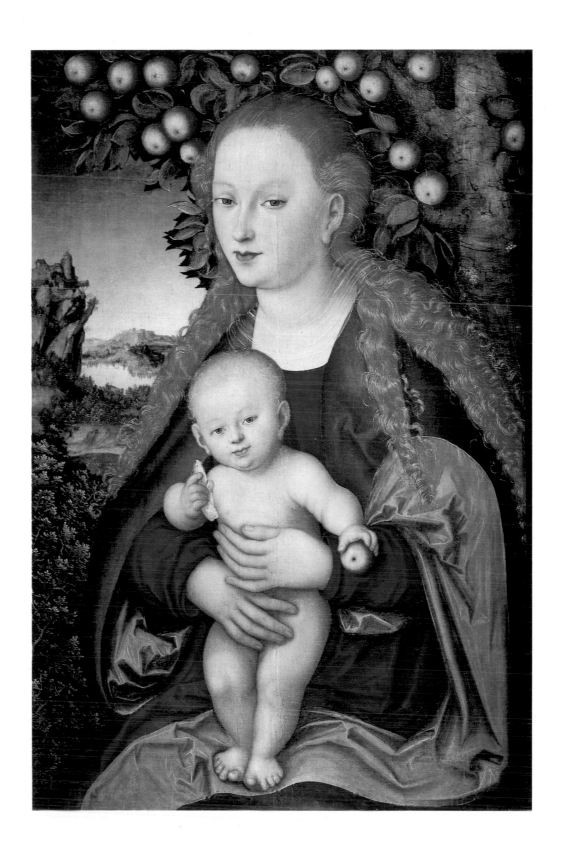

I spy
seventeen birds

17

Pablo Picasso, *The New Year*

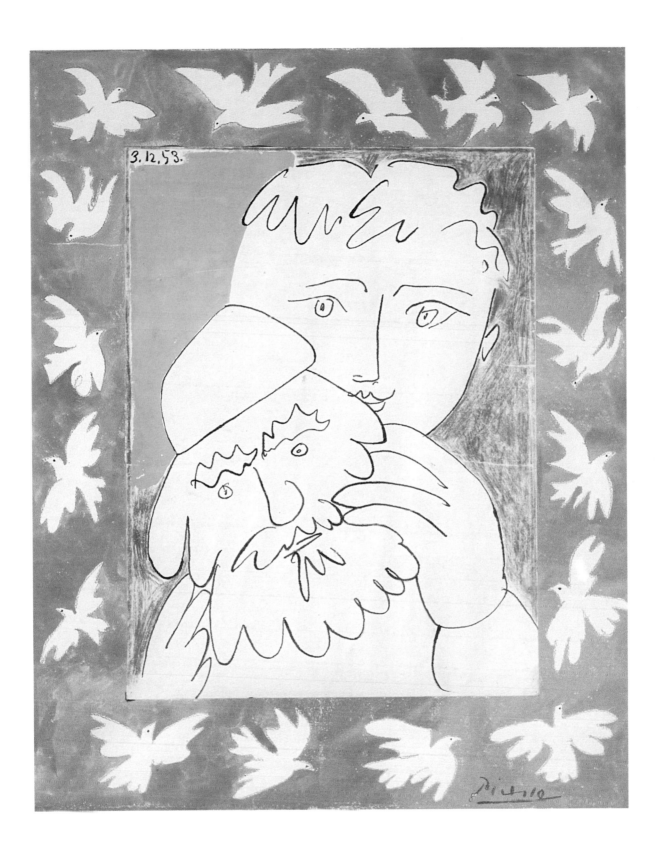

I spy
eighteen cherries

18

Georg Flegel, *Still Life*

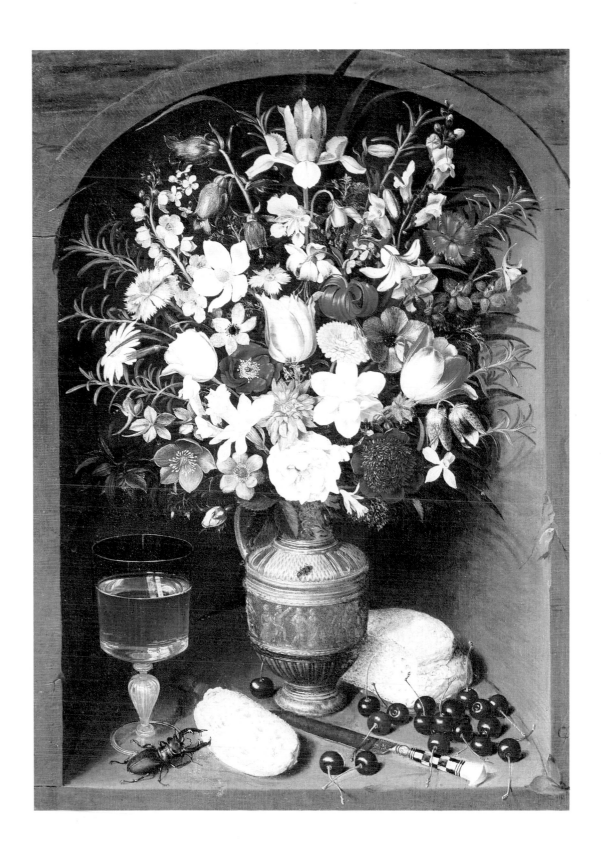

I spy
nineteen stars

19

Robert Indiana, *The American Dream I* (1961)

I spy
twenty angels

20

Sandro Botticelli, *Mystic Nativity*

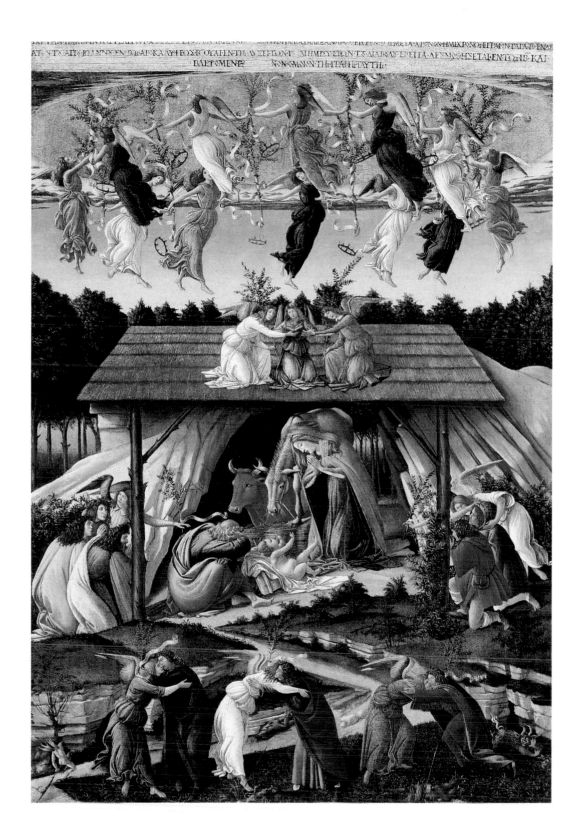

I Spied Numbers in Art...

1 one fly
Swabian School (15th century),
Portrait of a Woman of the Hofer Family
The National Gallery, London

2 two eyes
Karel Appel (born 1921), *Cry for Freedom* (1948)
Stedelijk Museum, Amsterdam

3 three puppies
Paul Gauguin (1848–1903), *Still Life with Three Puppies* (1888)
The Museum of Modern Art, New York, Mrs. Simon Guggenheim Fund

4 four fish
Henri Matisse (1869–1954), *Goldfish* (1911)
Pushkin Museum, Moscow

5 five eggs
Jan van Huijsum (1682–1749),
Flowers in a Terracotta Vase (1736–1737)
The National Gallery, London

6 six ducks
Utagawa Kuniyoshi (1797–1861), *Boat Trip in Winter* (about 1853)
Van Gogh Museum, Amsterdam

7 seven circles
Wassily Kandinsky (1866–1944), *Swinging* (1925)
The Tate Gallery, London

8 eight boats

Vincent Van Gogh (1853–1890), *Boats on the Beach* (1888)
Van Gogh Museum, Amsterdam

9 nine children

Studio of Peter Paul Rubens (1577–1640),
The Gerbier Family (about 1630)
The Royal Collection, St. James's Palace, London

10 ten hens

Sir Stanley Spencer (1891–1959), *St. Francis and the Birds* (1935)
The Tate Gallery, London

11 eleven hares

Unknown artist, *The Emblem of the Hare*
from *Le Livre de la Chasse* (about 1405–1410) by Gaston Phébus
Bibliotèque Nationale, Paris

12 twelve squirrels

Abu'l Hasan (17th century), *Squirrels in a Plane Tree* (about 1610)
The British Library, London

13 thirteen singers

Thomas Cooper Gotch (1854–1931), *Alleluia* (exhibited 1896)
The Tate Gallery, London

14 fourteen soldiers

Henri Rousseau (1844–1910), *Artillerymen* (about 1893–1895)
The Solomon R. Guggenheim Museum, New York,
Gift of Solomon R. Guggenheim

15 fifteen hands and feet
Fernand Léger (1881–1955),
Divers on a Yellow Background (1941)
The Art Institute of Chicago, Gift of Mr. and Mrs. Maurice Culberg

16 sixteen apples
Lucas Cranach the Elder (1472–1553),
Madonna and Child under an Apple Tree
Hermitage Museum, St. Petersburg

17 seventeen birds
Pablo Picasso (1881–1973), *The New Year* (1953)
Saint-Denis Musée d'Art et d'Histoire, Paris

18 eighteen cherries
Georg Flegel (1566–1638), *Still Life*
Private Collection

19 nineteen stars
Robert Indiana (born 1928), *The American Dream I* (1961)
The Museum of Modern Art, New York, Gift of The Larry Aldrich Foundation Fund

20 twenty angels
Sandro Botticelli (about 1445–1510), *Mystic Nativity* (1500)
The National Gallery, London

A C K N O W L E D G M E N T S

The author and publishers would like to thank the galleries, museums, private collectors,
and copyright holders who have given their permission to reproduce the pictures in this book.

Swabian School, *Portrait of a Woman of the Hofer Family;*
Jan van Huijsum, *Flowers in a Terracotta Vase;*
Sandro Botticelli, *Mystic Nativity,*
The Trustees, The National Gallery, London.

Karel Appel, *Cry for Freedom* © Karel Appel
c/o De Tulp Pers 1993/N.V. Koninklijk Bijenkorf Beheer.

Paul Gauguin, *Still Life with Three Puppies,* oil on wood, 91.8 x 62.6 cm.,
photograph © 1992 The Museum of Modern Art, New York.

Henri Matisse, *Goldfish* © Succession H. Matisse/D.A.C.S. 1993,
photograph: Bridgeman Art Library, London.

Utagawa Kuniyoshi, *Boat Trip in Winter;*
Vincent Van Gogh, *Boats on the Beach,*
Vincent Van Gogh Foundation/Van Gogh Museum, Amsterdam.

Wassily Kandinsky, *Swinging*
© A.D.A.G.P., Paris and D.A.C.S., London 1993.

Studio of Peter Paul Rubens, *The Gerbier Family* © H. M. The Queen.

Sir Stanley Spencer, *St. Francis and the Birds*
© Estate of Stanley Spencer 1993, all rights reserved D.A.C.S.

Abu'l Hasan, *Squirrels in a Plane Tree,* by permission of the British Library.

Thomas Cooper Gotch, *Alleluia,* photograph: John Webb.

Henri Rousseau, *Artillerymen,* photograph: David Heald
© The Solomon R. Guggenheim Foundation, New York, 1993.

Fernand Léger, French, *Divers on a Yellow Background,*
photograph courtesy of The Art Institute of Chicago/© D.A.C.S. 1993.

Lucas Cranach the Elder, *Madonna and Child under an Apple Tree,*
photograph: Bridgeman Art Library, London.

Pablo Picasso, *The New Year* © D.A.C.S. 1993.

Georg Flegel, *Still Life* © Christie's 1993.

Robert Indiana, *The American Dream I,* oil on canvas, 183 x 152.7 cm.,
photograph © 1992 The Museum of Modern Art, New York.

Cover picture: Henri Matisse, *Goldfish* (1911)
Title page picture: Henri Rousseau, *Artillerymen* (about 1893–1895)

Compilation and text copyright © 1993 by Lucy Micklethwait
The author asserts the moral right to be identified as the author of the work.
First published in Great Britain in 1993 by HarperCollins Publishers Ltd.
First published in the United States in 1993 by Greenwillow Books.
All rights reserved. No part of this book may be reproduced or utilized in
any form or by any means, electronic or mechanical, including photocopying,
recording, or by any information storage and retrieval system, without
permission in writing from the Publisher. Inquiries should be addressed to
Greenwillow Books, a division of William Morrow & Company, Inc.,
1350 Avenue of the Americas, New York, New York 10019.
www.williammorrow.com
Printed in Singapore

The Library of Congress has cataloged the Greenwillow Books edition of
I Spy Two Eyes as follows:
Micklethwait, Lucy.
I spy two eyes : numbers in art /
devised and selected by Lucy Micklethwait.
p. cm.
Summary: Uses the subjects of well-known paintings to
introduce the numbers from one to twenty.
ISBN 0-688-12640-5 (trade)
ISBN 0-688-12642-1 (lib. bdg.)
1. Counting—Juvenile literature.
[1. Counting. 2. Art appreciation.] I. Title.
QA113.M5 1993
513.2'11—dc20 [E]
92-35641 CIP AC

3 5 7 9 10 8 6 4
First Mulberry Edition, 1998
ISBN 0-688-16158-8